WINSTON
In the City

by Liam O'Donnell   Illustrated by Dan Hatala

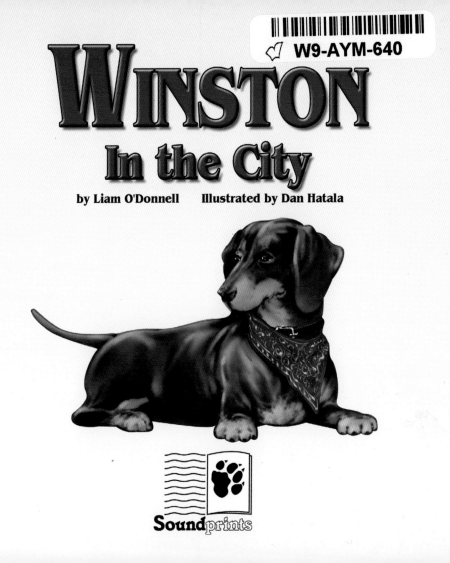

Soundprints

4

It's morning in the city! The streets are alive with sounds. Horns honk, engines rumble and bells clang. In an apartment high above the noise, a dog named Winston yawns and stretches.

Winston is a Dachshund and he is excited—today he is spending the day with his best friend, Hillary.

The two friends have lived together since Winston was a puppy. That was a long time ago, and Winston is now becoming an old dog.

Hillary is still asleep when Winston trots into her room. She doesn't wake up when he walks up to the bed, but a wet lick on her cheek will change that!

"Winston!" Hillary cries as she gives her best friend a cuddle.

Soon, Hillary is out of bed. She throws on some exercise clothes and is ready to take Winston to the park. Winston may be getting old, but he still enjoys his early morning walks!

After a long walk around the park, Winston is hungry!

Back at home, Winston eats a healthy breakfast while Hillary changes. After a final lick of his bowl, Winston is ready to hit the town. He will ride in his special carrier bag!

From the taxi window, Winston watches the city move around him. Hillary holds him carefully by his leash in case the taxi brakes too quickly.

Sidewalks swim with people coming and going, while roads crawl along with cars stopping and starting. Bike couriers weave through the stalled traffic like fishes swimming through water. The city is alive and Winston is excited to be in the heart of it!

13

At the café, Hillary's friends Angela and Charlotte are already sipping coffee. Winston likes this café because the owner always has tasty treats for his favorite dogs.

Winston isn't happy because he must share his treat with Charlotte's dog, Pasha. Pasha is a young puppy with too much energy for Winston. Pasha always wants to play, but Winston would rather eat his treat in peace.

After Hillary, Charlotte and Angela finish their food, it's time to leave. As Charlotte and Pasha dash off, Winston gives the poodle puppy a farewell bark.

Hillary, Angela and Winston walk through the city. Soon Winston's little legs grow tired. Thankfully, Hillary has her pet carrier bag and Winston gets a dog's-eye view of the bustling city!

Hillary and Angela take Winston to the dog groomer, where Winston has an appointment for a bath and nail trim. A few doors up is the beauty salon. Hillary and Angela arrive just in time for their appointments.

Brushes brush, clippers clip and blow dryers dry, making the three friends look their best.

After his fur is scrubbed and his nails are trimmed, Winston feels like a million doggie biscuits! He curls up and watches a playful puppy.

Just a few doors away, Hillary and Angela are buying new outfits.

Winston is snoozing when Hillary and Angela return to the groomer. He doesn't wake up when Hillary walks across the salon, but a kiss on the nose will change that!

On their way home, Angela pops into the grocery store to pick up food for dinner, leaving Winston and Hillary outside to admire their new looks in the store window.

Back at Hillary's apartment, Hillary and Angela try on their new clothes as delicious lasagna bakes in the oven. Suddenly, Winston's nose twitches at the smells coming from the kitchen. Something is not right.

Black smoke streams from the oven. The dinner is burning! Winston barks loudly, warning his friends.

Angela pulls the smoking lasagna from the oven. The dinner is ruined, but Winston is a hero. Hillary may be a great shopper, but she is a terrible cook!

Burnt lasagna won't ruin a day with good friends. Hillary orders pizza, and soon they are munching on pepperoni slices and watching their favorite TV show. Pizza isn't good food for dogs, so Winston gets a doggie biscuit for his heroic barking.

After dinner, Angela leaves. Winston and Hillary curl up on the couch and watch TV. Soon, both Hillary and Winston are sound asleep.

Outside, the streets are alive with sounds. Horns honk, engines rumble and bells clang. In the apartment high above the noise, Winston dreams of busy sidewalks and sunny cafés. The day is over, but tomorrow will bring more adventures for this downtown dog.

PET HEALTH AND SAFETY TIPS

• Pets age much faster than humans and require special care when they become seniors. On average, small-breed dogs can be considered to enter their senior years at age ten, medium-breed dogs at age eight and large-breed dogs at age seven. Most cats are considered senior pets at age ten.

• Strong preventive care programs, especially for older pets, help your veterinarian monitor your pet's changing needs and test for age-related health problems such as gum disease, arthritis, diabetes, and heart disease.

• Watch for subtle behavioral changes as your pet ages, such as reduced activity, limping or stiffness, loss of vision or hearing, or changes in eating habits. By diagnosing a health problem early, your veterinarian can better help you manage the condition.

• When taking your dog out in a vehicle, restrain it inside a properly sized pet carrier to keep it safe from sudden stops or turns.

GLOSSARY

Trot: A movement that is between a walk and a run.

Courier: A person who delivers mail and packages.

Café: A small restaurant that usually serves coffee.

A REAL-LIFE PET TALE

Moose the Dachshund is a city dog that sometimes thinks he's a squirrel. Moose lives in New York City with his friends Delaney and Michael. When they go for a walk in the park, Moose chases after squirrels and tries to climb the trees just to be like them! Moose enjoys playing fetch with Delaney in their apartment, but when Moose gets the ball he hides it under the couch, so Delaney does most of the fetching. Moose has a fancy collar and ID tags he wears when he's not on his leash. When he isn't pretending to climb a tree or hiding rubber balls, you may find Moose splashing in the bathtub.